TINY TERRORS

PUFFER FISH

JILL KEPPELER

PowerKiDS press

Published in 2024 by The Rosen Publishing Group, Inc.
2544 Clinton Street, Buffalo, NY 14224

Portions of this work were originally authored by Autumn Leigh and published as *Deadly Puffer Fish*. All new material in this edition was authored by Jill Keppeler.

Editor: Dwayne Hicks
Book Design: Michael Flynn

Photo Credits: Cover Grisha Bruev/Shutterstock.com; (series background) Ruswantodarkness/Shutterstock.com; p. 5 Jeffry Surianto/Shutterstock.com; p. 6 SaltedLife/Shutterstock.com; p. 7 Ana Krasavina/Shutterstock.com; p. 9 Dan Olsen/Shutterstock.com; p. 10 Ron Kuenitz/Shutterstock.com; p. 11 RaikHoff/Shutterstock.com; p. 13 Dmitry Rukhlenko/Shutterstock.com; p. 15 Jerry Widjojo/Shutterstock.com; p. 17 Jolanta Wojcicka/Shutterstock.com; p. 19 Isto Adhimas/Shutterstock.com; p. 21 TheNUshutter/Shutterstock.com.

Cataloging-in-Publication Data

Names: Keppeler, Jill.
Title: Puffer fish / Jill Keppeler
Description: New York : Powerkids Press, 2024. | Series: Tiny terrors | Includes index, glossary, and bibliographic information
Identifiers: ISBN 9781642826333 (pbk) | ISBN 9781642826340 (library bound) | ISBN 9781642826357 (ebook)
Subjects: LCSH: Puffers (fish)– Juvenile literature
Classification: LCC QL618.7 2023 | DDC 597.16-dc24

Manufactured in the United States of America

CPSIA Compliance Information: Batch #CSPK24. For Further Information contact Rosen Publishing at 1-800-237-9932.

CONTENTS

FUNNY FISH

Puffer fish can look funny. They can puff themselves up until they look like a ball, and they have big eyes. They even sometimes look like they're smiling. And although they live in the water, they're not great swimmers.

However, these funny fish have a secret. Most of them make a strong poison that tastes very bad. It can even kill some animals that might dare to eat them. That includes humans! Many also have **spiky** skin that makes them hard to eat.

DEADLY DETAILS

There are about 90 species, or kinds, of puffer fish in the family Tetraodontidae. Members of the family Diodontidae are sometimes also called puffer fish.

A puffer fish's spikes make it hard for animals to get a good bite.

A PUFFER'S HOME

Puffer fish live in warmer waters, many in **tropical** regions that form a band around the **equator**. They often live in the seas, many near the coast but some in deeper waters. However, some species live in freshwater, including rivers, all or most of the time. Still others live in places where saltwater and freshwater mix.

While many puffer fish live in the seas as shown here, some live in rivers such as the Nile, Congo, and Malagarasi Rivers in Africa.

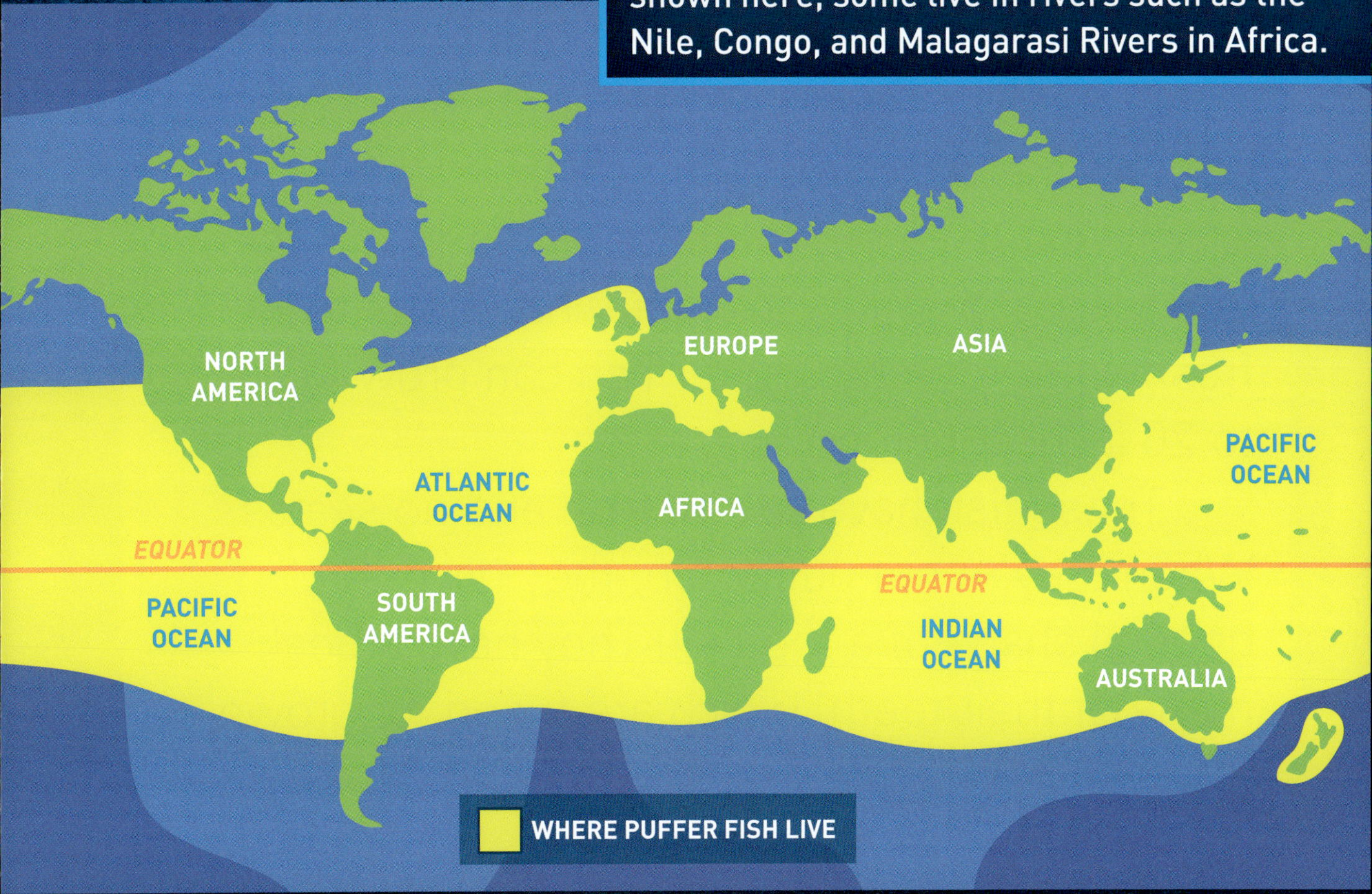

Many times, puffer fish will live around coral reefs. They'll eat other small fish and creatures that also live nearby.

BIG AND SMALL

Puffer fish come in many sizes, but most of them are fairly small. The Malabar puffer fish is only about 1.5 inches (3.8 cm) long (or less) when it's grown. On the other hand, the giant freshwater (or mbu) puffer fish can grow to be up to 26 inches (66 cm) long.

These fish have **tough** skin and no scales. When they're not puffed up, they have the general shape of a football! They have a beak made of their teeth, which are fused, or grown, together.

DEADLY DETAILS

Puffer fish can come in many different colors. They may have stripes or spots.

Congo puffer fish live in the Congo River in Africa. They're also called potato puffers!

THE PUFFER LIFE

Puffer fish can live about 10 years. They can **mate** and produce eggs after about five years. Puffer fish eggs are round and very light. They will float on the water until they **hatch**. This only takes a few days.

Baby puffer fish are very small. In fact, you probably couldn't even see them right after they hatch. They grow fast, however, and will quickly look like small versions, or types, of adult puffer fish. They'll join the adults when they're big enough.

People may think that Malabar puffer fish are baby puffers. They're just small!

FISH FOODS

Puffer fish use their beak to crack open the shells of their **prey**. Their favorite foods include crabs and clams. Sometimes they also eat **algae**. Different species may eat different things. They may also eat other small fish.

They can be sneaky hunters. Puffer fish lie in wait for prey to move by, or they'll swim up on prey and surprise it. They're not strong swimmers, but they can be fast just long enough to catch prey!

DEADLY DETAILS

Puffer fish that live in **captivity** may eat anything they can fit in their mouth.

Some kinds of puffer fish have beaks that never stop growing. They wear them down on their prey's shells. In captivity, they may need to have their beaks trimmed.

HOW TO PUFF

If they're bothered, puffer fish may suddenly become very round, blowing up like a fishy balloon. Their skin and stomach can **stretch** a lot. The fish will suck air or water into its stomach and puff up. It can swell to several times its original size.

Puffing up like this makes puffer fish very hard for other animals to eat. If they have spines, their spines will stick out too. They make a very uncomfortable mouthful!

DEADLY DETAILS

There are a few kinds of fish that can safely eat puffer fish. Most of them are sharks.

If a predator tries to eat this spiky snack, it might choke!

TETRAODONTOXIN

A toxin is a poison made by a living creature. Puffer fish have a particularly strong toxin called tetraodontoxin (or tetrodotoxin). It's partly in their skin but mostly in their organs, which are parts of the body that have a particular function, or job. This toxin makes them taste bad to some animals—and to others, it makes them very deadly.

Scientists think that tiny creatures called bacteria, which live in the puffer fish's body, make the toxin. They may get these bacteria from other animals they eat.

DEADLY DETAILS

There's enough toxin in one puffer fish to kill about 30 adult humans. There's no antidote, or way to stop the toxin.

If you're ever swimming in tropical waters and see a puffer fish, don't go near it! Most of its poison is inside, but if it pricks you with its spikes, you could be in big trouble.

PUFFERS AND PEOPLE

Puffer fish are wild animals, but some people keep them as pets. They may need pricy food and special places to live. Sometimes they can be dangerous to their owners and to other pets in the home! They're not for beginning fish owners.

Some species of puffer fish are threatened, or in danger, because of the loss of their habitat, or natural home. Some are also in danger of overfishing either for the pet trade or for eating by humans.

DEADLY DETAILS

Sometimes wild puffer fish are pulled from their homes and sold into the pet trade. This isn't good for the fish or the natural world.

People can be **responsible** puffer fish owners, but they need to know how to care for their pet.

A DANGEROUS MEAL

People eat some kinds of puffer fish. This dish, called fugu, is mainly known in Japan. Cooks who can make it must have years of special training. They must carefully cut out the toxic parts of the fish. If they do anything wrong in preparing it, the person eating it can die!

About 20 minutes to two hours after eating toxic fugu, a person will start to have symptoms, or signs, including dizziness, headache, and stomach pains. Then, paralysis sets in. This means the person won't be able to move—or breathe.

DEADLY DETAILS

A meal of fugu can cost hundreds of dollars. Even though it's dangerous, some people love how it tastes.

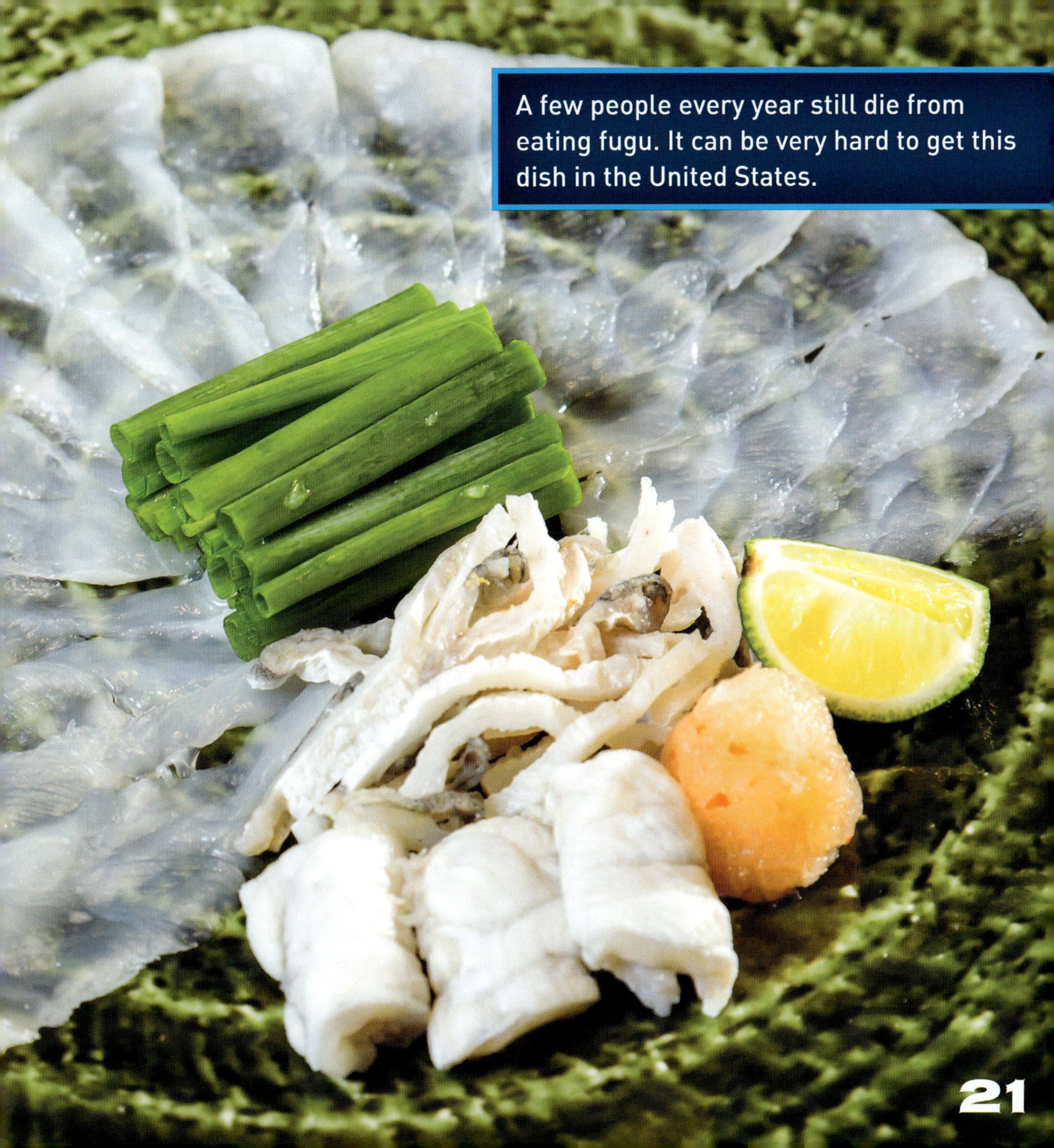

A few people every year still die from eating fugu. It can be very hard to get this dish in the United States.

GLOSSARY

algae: Simple plants with no leaves or stem that grow near water.

captivity: For an animal, the state of living somewhere controlled by humans—such as in a zoo or an aquarium—instead of in the wild.

equator: An imaginary circle around Earth that's an equal distance from the North Pole and the South Pole.

hatch: To break open or come out of.

mate: To come together to make babies, or one of two animals that come together to produce babies.

prey: An animal hunted by other animals for food.

responsible: Able to be trusted to do what is right.

spiky: Having spikes, or sharp points.

stretch: To become extended.

tough: Strong and not easily broken.

tropical: Warm and wet.

FOR MORE INFORMATION

BOOKS

National Geographic Kids. *Weird but True: Ocean*. Washington, D.C.: National Geographic, 2021.

Rose, Rachel. *Puffer Fish*. Minneapolis, MN: Bearport Publishing, 2023.

Shea, Therese M. *Pufferfish*. New York, NY: Gareth Stevens Publishing, 2018.

WEBSITES

Fifteen Types of Freshwater (and Saltwater) Pufferfish
a-z-animals.com/blog/15-types-of-freshwater-and-saltwater-pufferfish/
Learn more about some of the many kinds of puffer fish on this website.

Pufferfish
kids.nationalgeographic.com/animals/fish/facts/pufferfish
National Geographic Kids provides more information about puffer fish.

INDEX